ON THE STORY SEA

On the Story Sea
Hardie Grant Egmont
Ground Floor, Building 1, 658 Church Street
Richmond, Victoria 3121, Australia
www.hardiegrantegmont.com.au

A CiP record for this title is available from the
National Library of Australia.

Text copyright © 2015 Danny Parker
Illustrations copyright © 2015 Guy Shield
Series design copyright © 2015 Hardie Grant Egmont

Design by Stephanie Spartels
Typeset by Ektavo

1 3 5 7 9 10 8 6 4 2

Printed by McPherson's Printing Group, Maryborough, Victoria

The paper this book is printed on is certified against the
Forest Stewardship Council® Standards. FSC® promotes
environmentally responsible, socially beneficial and
economically viable management of the world's forests.

ON THE STORY SEA

DANNY PARKER
illustrated by Guy Shield

hardie grant EGMONT

CHAPTER ONE

It was the weekend, and Lola was going to a fancy-dress party.

But she had nothing to **wear** to a fancy-dress party!

She did have an old princess dress in the back of her closet.

But when Lola dug it up, she saw a big square cut out from the front of it.

Lola smiled. *Oh, that's right!* She'd cut it out to make a blanket for her toys. She didn't really like princesses these days, anyway.

Hunting around in her cupboard, she found some long stripy socks, and an old pair of jean shorts that she had almost grown out of.

She also found some of her mum's old scarves, and a belt.

It was **hopeless**!

Just then, her brother Nick looked into her room. 'What are you going to wear to the party?' he asked.

Lola shrugged.

'I know,' Nick snorted, 'you can pretend you're one of the ugly sisters from *Peter Pan*.'

Lola rolled her eyes.

'Or you could go as the ugly duckling from *Where the Wild Things Are!*' he said gleefully.

Then he bounded off down the stairs.

'You're muddling up your stories!' Lola called after him.

She slumped onto her bed next to her favourite toy, Buddy.

Buddy was a learn-to-dress clown, with lots of zippers and poppers, buckles and buttons.

'Easy for you,' she told him. 'You could just go as yourself. A clown!'

Lola was tired of looking for a costume. And anyway, the party was hours away.

She had **much** better things to do.

At the end of the bed was
her toy box. But this was no
ordinary toy box. Oh *no*.

This was Lola's **magical** toy box.

Lola picked up Buddy and
climbed inside her toy box.
Then she carefully closed the lid.

The toy box filled with light and
started to shake. Lola held onto
Buddy as they jiggled around
like a baby's rattle.

She squeezed her eyes shut.

Then, as suddenly as it had started, the shaking stopped. The lights went off again. Everything was still.

Lola took a deep breath, opened her eyes, and climbed out.

She had climbed **into** her toy box, but she had climbed **out of** …

CHAPTER TWO

She had climbed **out of** a magnificent treasure chest, on the deck of an enormous ship!

'Wow!' shouted Lola. 'Where in the Kingdom are we?'

She had to shout because the wind was blowing very loudly.

Buddy climbed out of the toy box behind Lola, clutching his hat with both hands.

'Bless my buttons!' he yelled. 'I think we are on a ship!'

Lola laughed. She wasn't sure she would **ever** get used to seeing her favourite toy come alive. Or hearing the funny way he spoke!

'I can see we are on a ship!' Lola shouted at Buddy. 'But where are we going?'

Her magic toy box always brought them to the Kingdom. It was a special place where toys came when they were not being played with at home.

Above Lola and Buddy were tall masts and huge sails. The sails were billowing in the wind.

'Let's get out of the wind,'
yelled Buddy, pointing to a small
wooden door. 'That's probably
the door to the ship's cabin.'

Lola and Buddy held hands and
leaned into the wind, taking one
step at a time towards the cabin
door.

But the wind was very strong.
It was tough going.

'This wind is amazing!'
Lola shouted.

Then, with no warning at all, the wind dropped. **Completely**.

Lola and Buddy tumbled onto the deck in a big heap of girl and toy.

Lola gasped as she sat up.

Right there, in front of her, was a pair of boots.

Big leather boots.

Big leather **pirate** boots!

Lola looked up. Wearing those big pirate boots was the most awesome pirate Lola had ever seen.

CHAPTER THREE

'Hello there,' said the pirate.

'I am Pirate Sal, at your service.'

Lola clambered to her feet.

She recognised Pirate Sal at once.
Lola had had a whole set of pirate
puppets when she was little.

She thought she'd lost them forever. Actually, she'd totally forgotten about them until … um, that very minute.

They must have been in the Kingdom all this time!

'Hello, Pirate Sal,' said Lola.

She wanted to give the pirate a huge cuddle, but she wasn't sure if Sal was the cuddling type of pirate.

Sal had golden hair and blue eyes, and earrings made of gold buttons.

She also had a very sharp-looking cutlass and a hook for a hand!

Pirate Sal gave Lola a nod.

'I've heard rumours that a real girl has been visiting the Kingdom,' Pirate Sal said. 'Welcome back!'

Word travelled fast in the
Kingdom.

But Lola was puzzled.

Pirate Sal sounded **friendly**.
She didn't sound at all
pirate-y.

'Is something wrong?' asked
Pirate Sal.

'Well,' said Lola, 'it's just that you
look like a pirate. But you don't
sound like a pirate.'

'That's because you wouldn't understand me if I spoke like a pirate,' Sal told her.

Lola frowned. She had heard pirates talk. She had seen pirate films. There had even been a day at school when everyone had tried to **speak** like pirates.

'I think I'd understand you,' she said.

'Very well,' the pirate replied.

Suddenly Pirate Sal's blue eyes seemed to flash, and she spoke again.

'Avast, ye land~lubbering squab and buffoon! Behold me bootstraps and canter on behind, d'ya hear? Afore the howlin' blizzard take ye over an' inta the drink!'

Lola and Buddy looked blankly at each other.

'OK, you're right,' Lola said with a grin. 'I didn't understand a **word** of that.'

'Not to worry,' said Sal, speaking normally again. 'I speak Land-Talk too. I was just saying, *Follow me before another gust of wind blows you overboard.*'

'Bust my buttons, Lola,' said Buddy, beaming with joy. 'Pirate Sal is the finest pirate on the Story Sea!'

Lola couldn't believe her luck. A pirate ship! This could be her best adventure yet.

CHAPTER FOUR

Pirate Sal led them to the front of the ship. Lola and Buddy held onto the rail as another huge gust of wind started to blow.

'Welcome aboard the *Eye Spy*!' shouted Pirate Sal. 'Fastest ship on the Story Sea.'

Lola couldn't believe how quickly the ship was sailing. It was very exciting, and it was also a teensy bit **scary**.

Buddy clung to her leg, so she picked up his soft little body for a cuddle.

Pirate Sal shouted at them to look ahead. Lola saw a large yellow shape **burst up** out of the water in front of them.

Then the shape was gone.

'Twist my toggle!' cried Buddy.
'What in the Kingdom was
that?'

Pirate Sal looked worried. 'We
don't know. We've been chasing
it for hours. I've never seen
anything like it before, and
I know these seas better than
any toy in the Kingdom.'

Moments later the giant yellow
thing jumped up out of the water
again, and then dived down.

This time, Lola got a good look. It was like a huge plastic whale. It had a big open mouth, but there were windows along the sides.

Lola had seen something like it before. Just last night, in fact, when she was having her bath!

Lola turned to Pirate Sal and said, 'I know what it is!'

Pirate Sal led them down to her cabin so they could talk where it was much quieter.

Lola, Buddy and Pirate Sal huddled together as Lola explained what they had seen.

'It's called a **submarine**,' said Lola. 'It travels under the water.'

Pirate Sal looked worried. 'A ship that goes under the water, eh?' she said. 'I've never seen one of those.'

Lola thought about the big open mouth on the submarine.

'Sometimes they're used to catch other boats. Or to attack them,' she said. 'And sometimes they secretly **scoop** things up from underwater!'

Pirate Sal was quiet for a moment, thinking.

'Come with me,' she said finally. 'I have something to show you.'

Pirate Sal opened a trap door in the floor.

Lola and Buddy followed her down the ladder and into the darkness below.

Lola looked around. Huge fishing nets hung from the walls. And she could see wooden treasure chests everywhere, lined up next to each other.

Pirate Sal opened a few of the treasure chests. Some were full to the top with paper. But many of the chests were empty.

'Usually these chests are all full,' Pirate Sal said. 'But someone has been stealing from me!'

CHAPTER FIVE

Pirate Sal pointed to the fishing
nets hanging from the walls.
'When we go fishing on the
Story Sea, we don't fish for fish.
We fish for stories.'

'How do you catch a story?'
Lola asked.

'You put a blank page into the water, and wait,' said Sal. 'After a while you pull the paper back out, and if you are lucky it has a story on it. Easy!'

Lola giggled. It sounded very magical, and much easier than trying to write a story all by yourself. Or going to the book shop to buy one!

'Usually we catch hundreds of stories. Old stories, new stories, funny stories. Look.'

Pirate Sal picked up a piece
of paper and handed it to Lola.
It said:

And he sailed off
through night and day,
and in and out of weeks
and almost over a year
to where the wild things are.

Lola smiled. It was one of her
favourite stories from when she
was little.

'You can keep it,' said Pirate Sal, grinning.

Lola popped the piece of paper into her pocket.

'The last few days, we've been fishing more than ever,' said Pirate Sal, 'but guess what?'

Buddy shrugged his floppy shoulders.

'No stories?' guessed Lola.

'That's right. So half our treasure chests are still empty,' said Sal.

What a mystery! thought Lola.

'Imagine a world without stories!' cried Buddy.

Lola thought about all her favourite books. The ones that made her feel good. And the scary ones, as well as the funny ones.

She even loved the sad ones.

Lola knew she had to do whatever she could to help Pirate Sal.

Whenever she needed to think, she paced around the room. This was one of those times.

Buddy took out his juggling balls. Whenever he needed to think, he started to juggle. It was a clown thing.

A mysterious submarine is seen in the Story Sea, thought Lola.

And stories are going missing …

Lola stopped pacing and looked across at Buddy and Sal.

'The submarine and the missing stories must be linked,' she said slowly. 'The submarine must be stealing the stories. But why?'

Buddy stopped juggling. 'Stories are very powerful, Lola,' he said. 'They are full of ideas. Often very clever ideas. That's why we treasure them.'

'Buddy's right,' said Pirate Sal. 'That's why we put the stories into books for everyone in the Kingdom to read.'

But who would want to steal the stories? wondered Lola. *Who in the entire Kingdom needs new ideas?*

She threw up her hands. It was so obvious.

'The Plastic Prince!' she cried.

The Plastic Prince was the ruler of Nevercalm. He ruled over the Almost Toys and was always up to no good.

What he wanted more than anything was control of the whole Kingdom.

'He is always after more power,' Lola reminded the others. 'And that's why it's a **plastic** submarine. It's from Nevercalm!'

CHAPTER SIX

'Well, tangle my laces, Lola,'
said Buddy. 'The Plastic Prince
stealing stories for more power?
It makes perfect sense! And a
plastic **subma-thingy** would
definitely be from Nevercalm.'

Lola looked thoughtful again. 'Have you seen any paper in the sea that shouldn't be there?' she asked Pirate Sal.

'Indeed we have!' replied Sal.

'The submarine must be fishing for stories!' said Lola. 'It's dropping paper into the sea, and then coming back to collect it all.'

'If this is the work of the Plastic Prince, we must stop that subma-thingy!' cried Pirate Sal.

They all went quiet, and Lola started pacing again.

Buddy started juggling again.

Lola tried to think of a plan. She knew that submarines were much faster than pirate ships. Ships needed the wind to sail, but submarines had powerful engines.

Lola suddenly felt nervous. What if the submarine captured all the stories?

If there were none left, then Pirate Sal and her puppet crew wouldn't be able to make books for the Kingdom's toys.

Come on, Lola, she told herself. *Think hard.*

She looked around. Treasure chests … fishing nets …

All at once, an idea popped into Lola's head. She looked up, her eyes sparkling.

Buddy dropped his juggling balls. He had seen that look on Lola's face before.

Lola had a **plan**.

CHAPTER SEVEN

Soon Lola, Pirate Sal and Buddy were back up on deck.

Sal ordered the ship's crew to bring up the treasure chests.

'But only the ones full of stories,' she said.

Lola watched the funny puppet pirates struggle to carry the heavy chests.

Soon the chests were all lined up, ready to go.

Pirate Sal was busy getting the fishing nets into place.

Buddy was standing next to Lola, watching it all.

'I hope this works,' he said. 'By my buttons, I do!'

Lola smiled. But she was nervous, too. It was a simple plan. Was it **too** simple?

If it went wrong, they would lose all the stories Pirate Sal had been keeping safe in the treasure chests.

They would be even worse off than they were now!

But Lola knew they had to try. They **had** to stop the Plastic Prince.

If he took **all** the great ideas from the world's stories, he would become even stronger. And then the whole Kingdom would be in danger!

Pirate Sal appeared at Lola's side. 'Everything is ready,' she said.

Together, Lola, Buddy and Pirate Sal walked over to the treasure chests.

'We should take one chest each,' said Sal. 'Are you ready?'

Buddy nodded.

Lola took a deep breath and nodded too.

'It's a splendid plan, Lola,' said Pirate Sal. 'Let's hope it works!'

CHAPTER EIGHT

Lola, Pirate Sal and Buddy
each opened a treasure chest.
Then, one by one, they started
throwing the pages into the
sea. The pages fluttered down
and landed in the water.

'When they get wet, the stories will leave the paper and return to float in the Story Sea,' called Pirate Sal.

Lola, Buddy and Sal worked quickly, throwing in more and more stories.

Soon the treasure chests were empty. Out at sea, a long line of pages drifted away from the ship.

They watched and waited.

Lola began to worry. Perhaps it wasn't such a good plan after all.

They watched and waited some more. *What if I've made a terrible mistake?* Lola thought.

Then, all of a sudden, it happened. There was a big splash, and the huge plastic submarine leapt out of the water!

Then it dived back down, sinking beneath the waves.

Lola felt her heart beating loudly. 'It's working,' she cried. 'It's working!'

The submarine jumped out of the water again.

It was moving quickly. And it was coming their way!

Each time the submarine jumped up they could see its big, open mouth scooping up the stories.

The first part of Lola's plan was working. But what would happen next?

In a few minutes, the submarine would be really close. The crew took their positions.

Pirate Sal climbed up the mast, ready to give the signal.

This was the scariest moment. Lola was holding her breath. This **had** to work.

Buddy touched her arm.

'It will be OK, Lola,' he whispered. 'I can feel it in my stuffing.'

Lola put her arm around her cuddly friend.

Then there was an almighty great SPLASH!

Lola gasped.

The submarine was right next to them!

It was so close that Lola could see in through the round windows.

The submarine was full of Almost Toys. So, they were right – the submarine *was* from Nevercalm!

'Release the nets!' yelled Pirate Sal.

The puppet pirate crew threw the fishing nets over the submarine.

The submarine was big and powerful. But it was also caught in Pirate Sal's huge fishing nets.

'Yippee!' Lola cried. 'We did it!'

CHAPTER NINE

Buddy started to turn cartwheels on deck as the pirate crew tied long ropes around the submarine.

Then they hoisted it high above the ship.

As the submarine swayed in the breeze, hundreds of pages started to fall from its giant open mouth.

More and more stories **poured** out.

Lola laughed in delight. She grabbed Buddy's mitten and danced beneath the falling pages.

Soon the deck of the ship was covered in stories.

Pirate Sal slid down on a rope from the mast, grinning.

Just then, Lola heard a rattling coming from the submarine above them. She grabbed Buddy and dived out of the way.

Just in time!

Four Almost Toys fell out of the submarine and onto the deck in a heap.

They were very **odd-looking**.

Lola always felt a bit sorry
for Almost Toys. They were
brightly painted, but they never
looked quite right.

And because they were plastic,
they didn't look, well, cuddly.
Not at all.

Pirate Sal strode over to Lola
and Buddy.

'We'll break up the plastic
subma-thingy,' said Pirate Sal.
'And we'll drop it in the drink!'

Buddy looked confused.

'The **drink** means the sea,' explained Lola.

'And then, these four toys can walk the plank!' said Pirate Sal.

Lola knew what that meant. It was a famous pirate punishment.

Enemies were made to walk along a wooden plank into the sea – and they never came out again.

'No,' said Lola. 'That's not fair!'

Pirate Sal looked at her,
surprised.

'Pirate Sal,' said Lola, 'it's just
not right. These Almost Toys
were only following orders.
We shouldn't hurt them.'

'But they were **stealing
stories**,' said Pirate Sal.

'Only because they were told to,'
said Lola firmly. 'Look at them.

Do you really think this was **their** idea?'

Pirate Sal looked over at the rather sad Almost Toys. Then she nodded slowly.

'You're right,' she said. 'We will keep them on board. Who knows? We might make pirates out of them yet!'

Lola laughed. The Almost Toys looked absolutely **nothing** like pirates.

Pirate Sal unclipped one of her gold button earrings and placed it in Lola's hand.

'This is a present to say thank you,' said Pirate Sal. 'And when you visit again, you will be known to all as **First Mate Lola**!'

Lola beamed. Buddy did another wonky cartwheel and landed on his head, his juggling balls rolling all over the deck.

Lola and Sal laughed. Then Lola gave Sal a cuddle. She was soft and furry, and she smelt of the sea.

'Thank you,' said Lola, holding the gold earring. 'I will treasure this.'

Then she had another idea. Reaching into her pocket, Lola pulled out the story Pirate Sal had given her earlier.

'Do you mind if I take a story back home with me?' Lola asked.

Pirate Sal beamed. 'Take your pick,' she said.

There were stories all around them, but Lola quickly made her choice.

Then, it was time to go home. Lola, Buddy and Sal walked over to where all the treasure chests were lined up.

There were so many that it took a while to find the right one!

But only one of the chests was Lola's magical toy box.

When they found it, Lola and Buddy said their goodbyes, and promised to return.

Then they climbed **into** the treasure chest. But Lola climbed **out of** …

CHAPTER TEN

Lola climbed **out of** her toy box. She was safe and sound, back in her bedroom.

She was happy to be home. But she was also sad that her adventure was over.

She gave Buddy a cuddle. He still smelt of the salty Story Sea. She popped him on her pillow.

Just then, she noticed that her cupboard door was still open.

Of course! The fancy-dress party. But now Lola knew exactly what to wear.

She grabbed the stripy socks and a scarf. She ripped the bottoms of her old jean shorts so they looked a little ragged.

There was just one more thing she needed. Pirate Sal's gold button earring!

Lola looked at herself in the mirror and laughed.

Looking back at her was **First Mate Lola!**

Then she heard Nick crashing up the stairs. He stopped when he saw Lola in her pirate outfit.

'Oh,' was all he could manage.

Lola knew that meant she
looked great.

'Nick,' she said, 'you were
getting your stories all muddled
up earlier. So I got you these.'

Lola gave Nick the two stories
she had brought back from
the Kingdom. He looked very
pleased indeed.

Mum called up the stairs, 'Lola,
have you got a costume yet?'

Lola laughed. There was only one answer to that question.

'Aye, aye, Captain!'

The Plastic Palace

NEVERCALM

Timberfields

Cuddleton Castle

The Story Sea

ABOUT THE AUTHOR & ILLUSTRATOR

Danny Parker is a writer and drama teacher who lives in Perth with his family. His previous books include *Tree* and *Parachute*. Danny is a keen juggler, singer and performer – just like Buddy!

Guy Shield is an illustrator who lives in Melbourne and is obsessed with drawing. When he was a kid, Guy loved building palaces and cities with his toys, just like Lola – and Nick!

When Lola is given an old toy
box, she discovers it's a magical
passageway ... to a world where
toys come to life!

Join Lola and Buddy on all
their adventures into the
toy box Kingdom and beyond!

You can follow Lola and Buddy into the Kingdom at
www.lolastoybox.com.au

Available in all good bookshops & libraries.